WRITTEN BY
DANIELLE NOVACK

ILLUSTRATED BY
PHYLLIS HARRIS

SCHOLASTIC INC.
NEW YORK TORONTO LONDON AUCKLAND SYDNEY MEXICO CITY NEW DELHI HONG KONG

For my two girls, Lucy and Maya.
—DN

For my nephew, Seth, with love.
—PH

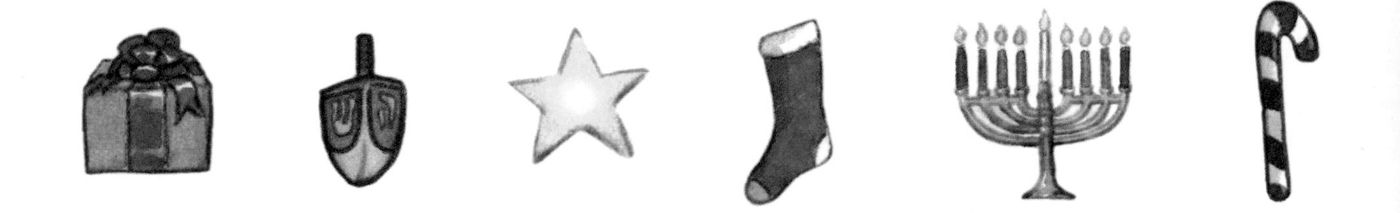

Library of Congress Cataloging-in-Publication Data

Novack, Danielle.
My two holidays : a Hanukkah and Christmas story / by Danielle Novack; illustrated by Phyllis Harris.
p. cm.
Summary: When Sam's classmates talk about which winter holiday each one celebrates, he gets embarrassed because his family enjoys both Christmas and Hanukkah.
ISBN 978-0-545-23515-0 (pbk.)
[1. Holidays–Fiction. 2. Schools–Fiction. 3. Christmas–Fiction. 4. Hanukkah–Fiction.]
I. Harris, Phyllis, 1962- ill. II. Title. III. Title: Hanukkah and Christmas story.

PZ7.N862My 2010
[E]–dc22 2010010728

ISBN 978-0-545-23515-0

10 9 8 7 6 5 4 3 2 1 10 11 12 13 14 15/0

Printed in the U.S.A. 40
First printing, September 2010

One cold December morning, Sam woke up and looked out his window. Everything was covered with white snow.

Winter was Sam's favorite time of year.

He loved sledding,

ice-skating,

building snowmen,

. . . and, of course, celebrating the holidays!

He was so excited that he jumped out of bed, got dressed, and ran downstairs.

In the living room, the Christmas tree sparkled with ornaments and twinkling lights. Sam had helped make strings of cranberries and popcorn for the tree.

In the kitchen, the silver menorah gleamed on the windowsill. Sam had helped polish the old menorah, which used to belong to his grandmother.

"Have some breakfast, Sam," said his mother.
"Did Santa come yet?" he asked.
"Not yet. There are a few more weeks to go until Christmas," his mother answered.

“What about Hanukkah?” Sam asked. “Can we light the menorah candles tonight?”

“No, Hanukkah is almost here, but it doesn’t start tonight,” said his mother.

He would just have to wait a little longer.

At Sam's school, the classroom had been decorated for the holidays.

Ms. Nancy played piano while the children sang "The Twelve Days of Christmas" and "I Have a Little Dreidel." Sam loved singing holiday songs. He knew all the words and sang in the loudest voice he could.

Then Ms. Nancy said, "Today we are going to learn about the holidays that people celebrate at this time of year. Some people celebrate Christmas and some people celebrate Hanukkah. Some people celebrate Kwanzaa. How does your family celebrate?"

“My family celebrates Christmas,” said Jack. “We put lights on our Christmas tree, and Santa slides down the chimney to leave us presents while we’re sleeping.”

"My family celebrates Hanukkah," said Maya. "We light the menorah every night for eight nights and play dreidel."

As each child described their special holiday, Sam didn't feel so excited anymore. He started to feel nervous and confused. All the other kids had just one holiday. Why didn't he?

Finally, it was his turn. “How do you celebrate, Sam?” asked Ms. Nancy. Sam looked around the room. His mouth was dry and his hands were clammy.

"Which one is it?" asked Jack. All the children stared at him, waiting for an answer. His face felt hot. He was too embarrassed to say he celebrated two holidays.

“I . . . I . . . I . . .” Sam stammered, and he ran into the bathroom. He stayed there for a long time.

When he came out, the class was doing arts and crafts. He was very quiet until it was time to go home.

"I don't want to go to school anymore," Sam told his mother.
"What happened?" she asked.

Sam told her about the teacher's question and about hiding in the bathroom.

"I wish we just celebrated one holiday. It's weird to have two."

Sam's mother hugged him. "Actually, many people celebrate both Christmas and Hanukkah. It's very special to have two holidays."

Then she explained, "Your dad is Christian and he has always celebrated Christmas. We decorate the tree and hang stockings by the fireplace. Santa will leave you lots of presents, and Nana and Papa will come for turkey dinner on Christmas Day."

"I love Christmas," said Sam.

"I am Jewish," continued his mother, "so I have always celebrated Hanukkah. This menorah has been in our family for generations. My grandmother gave it to my mother. Then my mother gave it to me. Every year, we light the candles for eight nights. We give one another presents, play dreidel, and eat latkes—potato pancakes fried in oil—with applesauce and sour cream."

"I love latkes!" said Sam.
"And I love Hanukkah too."

Sam smiled as his mother hugged him. "You see," she said, "Christmas and Hanukkah are about celebrating our love as a family. It's one of the things that makes our family special."

The next day, Sam marched into his classroom with his head held high. He did not feel embarrassed anymore. Sam sang the holiday songs in a loud, clear voice. Then Ms. Nancy said it was time for recess.

"Wait," said Sam. "Yesterday, I didn't get to tell the class how my family celebrates the holidays." All the kids looked at him. "Well, okay, Sam," said Ms. Nancy. "Go ahead."

A B C
COLORS
TEDDY
CAT
TIME
1 2 3

“My family celebrates Christmas AND Hanukkah,” said Sam.
“I get Santa AND latkes AND stockings AND a menorah!”
The kids were quiet. Then they started to smile.

Jack said, "That's really cool."
Maya said, "You are SO lucky."
Ms. Nancy said, "Thank you for
telling us about your two holidays."

After that, Sam felt great. He was so excited for the holidays. "It's okay to be a little different," Sam told his parents when he got home. "Celebrating Hanukkah and Christmas means more fun and lots of love. I can't wait for MY TWO HOLIDAYS!"